Awesome Adventures of

Miss Kitty

and Her

Woodland Friends

MarySue Peters

ISBN 978-1-0980-6198-2 (paperback)
ISBN 978-1-0980-6199-9 (digital)

Christian Faith Publishing, Inc.
832 Park Avenue
Meadville, PA 16335
www.christianfaithpublishing.com

Printed in the United States of America

Completing this first book on my journey as a new writer has been a joy and fun as I fulfill a lifelong dream of writing my own book. I grew up an avid reader. This journey could not have been completed without the love and support of my dear wonderful husband, Claude Peters. I also owe much thanks to my very supportive agent, Julie Sheppard, along with my publication specialist, Sarena Gray, and her editing staff. Kudos to the illustration staff for giving life to all my whimsical characters. And last, but not least, much love goes to Miss Kitty herself, who is one of four cats and a dog we share our home with. She was my inspiration for this whole grand adventure.

Chapter 1

Miss Kitty Wakes

Miss Kitty wakes up and lazily stretches and yawns. It is early morning, very early. A new day to play. A new day to explore. But most importantly, a new day for a new breakfast.

"I am very hungry when I wake up so early."

But no worries, it's too pretty a day to be worried. The sun is barely above the treetops. The air is still filled with night chill. For now, Miss Kitty has one thing on her mind—food.

"I am very hungry," says Miss Kitty as she feels her stomach growl.

She jumps down from her red cushioned throne and gracefully steps across the porch to her food bowl.

Alas! It is empty!

"Oh my! I know I had some leftovers from supper last night when I went to sleep. I must have had a visit from Petey Possum during the night. He is very good at sneaking up here during the night and helping himself to my leftovers. As I inspect the whole bowl intently, I see that Petey has not left me one morsel, not one tiny crumb! He is very good at cleaning his plate—or anyone's plate—after each meal. He never leaves leftovers! I do believe Petey thinks he is a pig sometimes, not a possum. But since I am a lady, I always leave a few nibbles in my bowl. But it would be nice to return later to eat my own leftovers!"

Miss Kitty rolls to her side and begins her morning bath as she ponders her breakfast situation.

"A lady can never be too clean or take too many baths. After all, living outdoors causes my luscious coat to become quite dusty. For my breakfast choice, I could catch a fish in the pond, but I don't quite feel like having wet feet today. I could catch birds, but when I chase birds, the wind tickles my whiskers."

After much thinking over this dilemma of an empty food bowl, Miss Kitty finishes her morning groom. She decides the best way to handle this situation is to just sit tall, look pretty (as she always does), and sing out loud.

"I do have such a sweet voice."

Miss Kitty has many friends in her woods that enjoy her loud meows. But this morning she is only singing loud because she is hungry—very, very hungry.

Miss Kitty is not only a beautiful kitty with manners, but also a smart kitty. In a very short time, she learned that when she sings in her loudest voice, it causes the most wonderful thing to happen. Her voice made food appear! On the mornings that she chooses to sit and sing on this nice, cozy porch, before much time passes, the huge red door to her castle opens and out steps the Nice Lady with her breakfast.

"Since I am a polite kitty, I must thank her. So I walk over close to her legs and rub my soft fur against them and wrap my big fluffy tail around her ankles. It's wonderful to feel her scratch behind my ears. I purr loudly so she knows how happy I am to see her this beautiful morning. But then my stomach growls, and I am reminded of what she is holding—my breakfast! I run over to my food bowl and meow a very big thank you as she pours wonderful tiny pieces of fish, chicken, and beef into my bowl. As I eat my breakfast, I feel that just maybe this one time I shall leave no leftovers for Petey Possum."

Chapter 2

Tree Frog Trio

"Breakfast is so wonderful, fantastical, superlicious delicious!" Miss Kitty quickly decides as she daintily munches on each tiny piece. "No matter how much my tummy wants it all now, I am a lady and ladies never gobble it all at once. Oh dear, sometimes I do wish I were not a lady, then I could so enjoy my food faster! As I near the end of this beautiful morning meal, I realize I've almost finished every last bite. But I can't do that. I remember I shall leave a leftover. I decide to leave one tiny crumb. Surely one crumb may count as a leftover? Petey Possum may think different. But he won't be out and about till tonight."

Miss Kitty lazily stretches out in a sunny patch on her porch. It's time for another bath.

It is a good day, she thinks. *I have a warm spot to bathe in and a full tummy.* Almost too full, she realizes as a burp—a most tiny ladylike burp, of course— escapes her lips. Miss Kitty's ears twitch sharply as she hears three tiny giggles. Instantly, she knows exactly where the giggles are coming from. But she decides to ignore the giggles and continues her after-breakfast groom. Then she releases another burp, louder than the first, and immediately she hears the three tiny giggles again.

Well, I ignored their rudeness once, I will not ignore it a second time, she thinks.

She gracefully rises from her sunny spot, which is slowly moving away from her by now. She slowly slinks over to her red cushioned throne, jumps up on it, and poses herself regally. She pretends to ignore the giggles for a few minutes more as the sounds get louder. Then in a blink of an eye, she raises her head up high and stares straight up at the source of the tiny giggling sounds. She admonishes the source of the giggles with a fierce glare and twitches her fluffy tail.

But does this stop the gigglers from giggling? No! How dare they continue to giggle as she sits upon her red cushioned throne. Have they forgotten their manners?

The giggles are coming from the tree frog trio—Billy, Bobby, and Betsy—or better known to all in the woods as the trio teasers. She knows they will giggle and laugh at anyone. It's their nature to be happy and carefree. They haven't a care or worry in the woods. But to be the one laughed at is no fun at all, no fun indeed.

As she glares up at the trio perched sideways on the tall column, they stare back down at her as they hop over each other on their way down the column. The column is very tall. It seems to Miss Kitty to be as tall as the oldest tree in her woodlands.

The trio continues their game of hopscotch further down as they get closer to Miss Kitty. Miss Kitty's glare follows their track down the column. Hop by hop, jump by jump her glare doesn't waver. But as her tail stops twitching, her whiskers begin to twitch instead. Her whiskers twitch faster. Her whiskers give her away by the time the trio is at the bottom of the column. Now they are straight across from Miss Kitty and her twitching whiskers as she sits upon her red cushioned throne in her most regal pose. Her glare disappears as her whiskers twitch fast, very fast.

Why could it be? Then the trio realize that Miss Kitty is laughing at them! Her whiskers cannot hold in her laugh any longer. As she knows how the tree frog trio laugh and giggle at all in the woods, so do all in the woods laugh at their antics. Their giggles are very contagious. No one can stay mad at Billy, Bobby, and Betsy for long. No indeed!

But still, she thinks, *they need to be reminded of their manners.*

It surely may be funny to hear someone burp, even a lady such as Miss Kitty, but it is quite rude to giggle over it. So she tries to bring back her glare as she points her clawed paw toward the trio. Even though her glare is not as fierce as it was the first time, her outstretched clawed paw makes her point quite clear to the trio. They shouldn't have giggled at her burp and most definitely not again at her second burp! Even though the second burp was much funnier than the first burp! As she keeps her clawed paw pointed at the trio, she sharply tells the three to never ever giggle at her burps again. That is, if she should ever possibly emit another burp. She certainly doesn't plan to. If they do, punishment will be banishment from the tall column on which they love to hop and jump upon all day (for at least one day).

At this declaration, the tree frog trio hop on top of each other so as to stand taller in her regal presence and promise to never ever giggle at her burps again. That is, if she should ever burp again. But Miss Kitty does not see that as the trio stand on top of one another, their little toes are crossed together over each other in a knot, which means they may not be able to keep their solemn promise!

"Away with you silly three," says Miss Kitty. "I have important kitty business to attend to on this beautiful sunny morning. So hop away at once and don't hop back too soon. Go giggle at someone else this morn."

Off the trio race, each trying to outjump and outhop the other, all the while giggling at Miss Kitty's pretend anger.

Chapter 3

Freddy Fox

After she watches the tree frog trio hop away, she jumps down from her red cushioned throne. She strolls slowly to the edge of the porch and begins her descend down the many steps one at a time.

"I could easily jump the steps all at once," she says to herself. "But that display of exertion would be so unladylike!" So she continues her regal gait downward step by step. "But one day I shall jump them all at once when I am quite sure no one is watching. It is good to take a little stroll on such a grand morning as today. If I am lucky, I may even come across one of my woodland friends today. Then today would surely be a wonderful day."

Once off the last step, she gingerly walks across the crunchy gravel and crosses over to her giant bowl.

"My water bowl is so large that I am able to share it with all my woodland friends. I have heard the Nice Lady who brings me my wonderful tiny pieces of fish, chicken, and beef call my giant water bowl a strange name. She calls it fountain, whatever that is. I only know that it is very big and always full of clear cool water. It has many bowls, one on top of the other. The biggest bowl of cool water is the lowest and easiest to reach. The highest bowl near the blue sky is small and only reached by the birds. The same birds that I never chase for my breakfast."

She was nearing closer to her cool sip of water when all of a sudden out from behind a bush jumps Freddy Fox! He lowers his head, bares his teeth, and switches his tail! It takes a few seconds for her neatly groomed fur to settle back in place, for his surprise greeting had startled her. Then she calmly continues right past him and toward her giant water bowl.

"Oh, Freddy, quit playing around. It's too early to be out and about playing pranks on your friends. Come and join me for a cool sip of water."

Freddy sits downs and mopes, for he had so hoped to give Miss Kitty a good fright. He did for a few seconds, but she would never let on. Freddy is a very handsome bushy-tailed red fox. He's quite young. She has heard the Nice Lady call Freddy a kit. I do believe that has something to do with him being so young. But to all his friends here in the woods, he's just Freddy. Freddy Fox. Freddy's greatest joy in life is playing pranks on all his friends. All his friends are used to his pranks, but sometimes his pranks can be quite annoying. Sometimes we have to prank him back to show him it's not always fun. But Miss Kitty will save those stories for another time. When she reaches her giant water bowl, she easily jumps up on the edge and sits daintily, balancing on its edge.

She wonders who else in the woods might have a water bowl large enough to sit upon. She turns her head and sees Freddy still moping with his head hung low and his bushy tail tucked under his rump.

"Freddy, be a dear, please, and come join me up here on my water bowl. I'm quite alone up here and would enjoy your pleasant company."

Upon hearing that she is not mad at him for scaring her, his head lifts, his ears perk up, he uncurls his beautiful red bushy tail and in two jumps he is by her side on the water bowl.

"Miss Kitty, I am sorry for jumping out at you. I'll try to be good and not do it again. Well, at least not again today," he adds under his breath.

Miss Kitty tells Freddy what a wonderful day today will be.

"I've had a very nice delicious breakfast, two baths, a warm spot of sun to stretch out in on the porch."

As she sits on the edge of her huge water bowl, she proceeds to dip one dainty paw into the cool water, then she brings the paw up to her mouth to lick the water from her paw. For this is the way a lady sips her cool water.

But alas, Miss Kitty is not ready for what's about to happen next! Freddy Fox gives his great red bushy tail a big swish and pushes Miss Kitty right down into her own huge bowl of cool water! Oh, Freddy, will he never learn?

Miss Kitty lets out a horrendous screech as her beautiful coat of fur gets soaking wet. This is definitely not the kind of bath she had in mind today!

Freddy Fox takes off running as fast as his short legs will carry him. Miss Kitty swiftly climbs out of the huge water bowl, back upon the edge where she was before Freddy did this awful prank to her.

"Oh, Freddy! You just wait," she says to herself.

Chapter 4

"Sir How" the Owl

Poor Miss Kitty she is soaking wet, thanks to Freddy Fox! But Miss Kitty has no time to think about Freddy at this moment. She needs to dry herself off and re-groom her beautiful fur. The problem of Freddy can wait till later. But not much later! Miss Kitty has had enough water for the moment. She jumps down off the edge of her giant water bowl and tiptoes across the crunchy gravel over to a nice sunny spot she sees in the warm grass. She gently sits down on this spot she picked out and begins to groom herself from head to toes to the tip of her great fluffy tail, which is not so fluffy now as she looks at it.

"Oh, how horrible to be so wet all at once, all over!"

After she has finished smoothing out her gorgeous coat and getting each piece back in its proper place where it belongs, she stretches out on the warm grass. She's quite ready by now for a little snooze, or as some might say a catnap.

While she enjoys her nap, she starts to hear a familiar sound.

"How, how." A few minutes go by, then again, "How, how."

The noise gets closer, then even closer, then very close, and then right next to her ear. She hears it quite clearly.

"How, how!"

Miss Kitty opens one eye and looks up into the two large round horn-rimmed glasses of Sir How the owl.

"Go away, Sir How. I am busy drying my fur as I catnap. I've no time for your questions today."

Sir How replies in his nasal-toned voice, "I see my friend, Miss Kitty, is quite wet. But how did you get so wet?"

"Go away, please."

"I see one side of you will dry easily in the sun, but how will you dry the other side?"

"Go away, please," Miss Kitty repeats.

"How did you sleep last night? I hope well."

"Go away."

"How was your breakfast this fine morning? Tasty, I hope."

"Go away."

"How will you teach Freddy Fox not to do this again?"

At this last question, Miss Kitty opens both eyes and perks her ears up. At last, Sir How has a question that Miss Kitty wants an answer to. How would she teach Freddy Fox to behave himself? Sir How the owl is a very wise owl, but he is quite different from other owls in her woodlands, for he never asks the question of "who, who" as they do. He is much more inquisitive. He wants to know how things are done. He ponders things such as how the sun comes up, how the wind blows or how the rain falls down and not up.

Miss Kitty sits up from her catnap, stretches, and then rolls over to her other side.

"As you can see, Sir How, this is how I will dry my other side of fur. And to answer your question of how I became so wet, that was all because of Freddy Fox. He pushed me into my huge water bowl with his great red bushy tail. And yes, my breakfast was quite tasty. And yes, I slept very well last night between my patrol walks around our great woodlands."

Sir How the owl is all ears as he listens most intently to Miss Kitty's answers. For what good is a question if one does not listen to the answers? Miss Kitty is now fully awake. Finishing her glorious warm catnap is quite impossible now that Sir How the owl is perched on a twig only inches from her whiskers. He always sits very close to his listeners, for he is extremely farsighted. He can spot a snail on a tree branch far off in the neighboring woods. He's always on the prowl for a tasty snail. They are his favorite dessert. But to talk pleasantly with one of his many friends, he must sit very, very close to their nose. Miss Kitty often wonders why he bothers to even wear glasses. They don't seem to help. He has only told her, and no one else, that he wears the glasses because he is quite vain. He believes the glasses make him look as smart as the other owls in the woods. He thinks they are smarter because they ask "who" and he prefers to ask "how." Miss Kitty thinks he does not need glasses to appear smart, simply because he is smart. He is the smartest and most polite friend of all her friends in her great woodlands.

"My, my, Miss Kitty, how will you ever finish your wonderful catnap now that you are awake?"

That's an easy question for her to answer. "I will easily finish my catnap when you go away! I must dry my other side of fur in the sun as I nap. When I awake, I shall feel and look as good as new," she tells him.

"Oh yes, yes, Miss Kitty, that is a very good answer to my question." Sir How the owl turns his head to one side, spies a snail nearly two miles away on a log, and flies up and away toward his next dessert. He always prefers his dessert before his meal.

Chapter 5

The Wren Family

After a few more undisturbed hours of catnapping in the warm sun, Miss Kitty arises and stretches her long fluffy body out. As she stretches, she rolls side to side, wriggling during the process. She quickly decides that every piece of hair is dry and back in its proper place. She curls her tail up to scratch her itchy pink nose. She does so love to catnap in the warm grass, but it always makes her pink nose itch and twitch. She decides an itchy twitchy pink nose is a small price to pay for such a glorious nap in the warm sun. As she rolls over to a regal pose (it's quite a fact, that all of Miss Kitty's poses are regal), she eyes her red cushioned throne on the porch of her castle and decides that her next much-needed catnap shall be on her throne. So off she struts across the crunchy gravel. It is well that her castle is surrounded by this crunchy gravel, for it lets her know if any unwanted visitors are approaching.

As she passes by her giant water bowl, her hair bristles and whiskers twitch at the memory of her unexpected bath in the water bowl.

"It reminds me that I must decide on what to do about Freddy Fox. He must be taught a lesson about his naughty pranks."

On toward her porch she continues, when all of a sudden, a cascade of twigs and dust rain down upon her nicely groomed head. The downpour of twig dust causes her to jump up in the air with a fright. In an instant she lands back down on all four paws, shaking her head left to right, right to left as she sneezes several times. She tries to plop down in a regal fashion, but just how does a lady go about plopping regally, and with twig dust all over her head? Why, there's just no way to look regal while in such a state as she is in at the moment. This day is just not going as well as she had expected. As Sir How the owl would say, "How could such a beautiful day go so wrong?"

Miss Kitty stands and looks all around for the twig dust droppers. She has a good idea just who is responsible for this calamity. As her gaze continues to the top of her porch, she eyes the culprits!

"Just as I suspected," she growls.

The wren family has returned! Mr. and Mrs. Wren with four new babies in tow!

Oh dear, there go my peaceful catnaps while they are camped out above my throne at the top of the column. True, while they are nice neighbors, they are also quite a bit annoying and noisy and messy and clumsy. Why, just last summer, they were always dropping twig dust all over my nice red cushioned throne. Their children were constantly fighting over who got the biggest worm, they have no table manners, and they love to practice dive bombing accuracy while using my tail as a target! I was so hoping that this year the wren family would go to another condo vacation spot. But to be fair, she thinks, *they are very watchful.*

The wren family are selfish about the air space around their twig condo. They don't like to share it with any other birds. All six member of the wren family, when excited, can sound louder than a gaggle of geese, louder than a pen full of hungry pigs, louder than ten bullfrogs even! So Miss Kitty is really secretly glad when they return each year, even though they can be quite annoying at times.

Miss Kitty continues her trek to her red cushioned throne, all the while keeping a watchful eye for another shower of twig dust to come her way. Up the steps she gracefully struts, never once letting her beautiful tail touch a step. Before she reaches her throne, she casts a glance at her food bowl. It is empty again! Even the one tiny piece of leftover crumb is gone!

Well, first things first, she jumps up on her throne and begins, once again, to bath her dusty head. A lady does not eat while dirty! After a few minutes, she is spotless and shiny once again. All pieces of her beautiful fur are back in their proper places, and her fluffy tail is wrapped daintily around her paws.

She decides she must start another song of meows since her stomach is growling for lunch. Soon the Nice Lady appears at the red door with her wonderful tiny pieces of fish, chicken, and beef. Miss Kitty repeats her thank you of this morning by wrapping her soft silky tail around the ankles of the Nice Lady and purring her thanks. The Nice Lady picks Miss Kitty up in her arms and kisses the top of her head gently. Miss Kitty purrs louder, then wriggles to get down, back to her food bowl. She wants to eat now. She can be loved later on a full stomach.

Chapter 6

Dolly Doe

After a very filling and tasty lunch, Miss Kitty jumps back up on her red cushioned throne and begins her after-lunch bath. She's sure to wash every whisker, every paw, the back of her ears (as everyone should do daily), and every hair on her luscious fluffy tail.

Now I am ready for my after-lunch catnap, she thinks.

She settles down deeper into her red cushioned throne. She covers her long lashes with her bushy tail. Soon she is sound asleep. Little snores escape past her whiskers. Miss Kitty would be aghast to know she snores! She is sure proper ladies do not snore! The wren family are flying through the woodlands for afternoon exercise. The wren babies are very enthusiastic in life. They must see all, do all, annoy all—and have fun in the process! At least, they are busy elsewhere while Miss Kitty enjoys her after lunch catnap.

The afternoon winds down as Miss Kitty snoozes. She has had a very tiresome day. What with the dunk in her giant water bowl, then the twig dust fiasco! She does hope the day will have a much calmer end to it. She must get a good restful catnap all through the afternoon so she can prowl part of the night and watch over her woodlands for any unwelcome intruders.

As the afternoon drifts away closer to sunset, Miss Kitty stretches her long body fully out. Her whiskers twitch as she sniffs the air. She doesn't smell the moonvine yet. So it's not too late in the evening. Not time yet to prowl and protect her castle.

But it is time to eat, she realizes as her stomach reminds her it's been quite a while since she's had lunch. Off her throne she jumps quickly and strolls over toward her once-again empty food bowl.

"Oh, dear me! Did I forget to leave any leftovers! I must have, for it is too early for a visit from Petey Possum. He never visits me before the smell of moonvine is in the air."

She sat very straight and tall, head held high, ears up nicely, tail wrapped prettily around her paws and began her beautiful meow song. She sang very loud, for she was very hungry. It wasn't very long before the big red door of her castle opened and out stepped the Nice Lady with her evening meal. Wonderful, delicious tiny bits of fish, chicken, and beef! She wants to jump up toward her, hand holding my tiny bits of supper, but she does not for that would not be lady like. She simply thanks her with her beautiful sounds of meow and hugs her legs with her fluffy tail.

She scratches behind her ears (which, if you remember, are clean). She gives her a good-night kiss upon her head and promises her a tasty breakfast come morning. After Miss Kitty finish her supper, she is sure to leave a few tiny leftover bites for Petey Possum, for he is sure to come for a visit and a snack during the night.

Miss Kitty strolls over to the last small piece of sun that is left on the porch in which to sit and take her evening after-supper bath. She must look presentable on her prowl tonight through the woodlands, for she is sure to meet many of my friends in the woods.

The last of the day sinks below the farthest tree that Miss Kitty can see in the distance. Now is no time for a much-desired catnap. But perhaps she could sit and let one eye take a little nap. Miss Kitty curls up in that last small fading spot of warm sun and slowly closes one eyelid, then slowly before she can stop it, the other eyelid follows the first eyelid. Then and there Miss Kitty is fast asleep with a tummy full of tiny delicious bits of fish, chicken, and beef.

Luckily for Miss Kitty, it is a very short catnap. She is awakened by the scent of moonvine flowers, a delicious aroma that swiftly caresses her pink nose and causes her whiskers to gently twitch. The moonvine smell!

"Oh, dear me." She yawns as she comes fully awake and aware of how the night has covered her porch. "I must be on my way now," she says as she quickly, but daintily, trots down the steps to the crunchy gravel. Then she trots quietly and softly around the far side of the castle. As she swiftly glides through the darkness, she goes in, through, under, and between every bush, checking for unwanted guests. When she nears the backside of her castle, she slides under the biggest bush of them all. It is her favorite spot to hide under and watch the other woodland animals wander by. Some are friendly. Some are not so friendly.

As she lies low and quiet, she sees far across her domain to the outer edges of the woodlands. Her eyes follow a shadow outlined in the moonlight. The shadow moves slowly and is also very quiet. Behind the shadow she can see two more shadows following close. The three shadows are close enough together to seem almost as one. The shadows move out of the moonlight and seem to disappear. But she knows better. She knows the shadows are getting nearer and nearer to her bush and to her hiding under the bush! But Miss Kitty is not afraid. She is never afraid of her friends, and she can tell by the approaching scents that these three shadows are friendly.

Miss Kitty stays very still and quiet. She twitches not a whisker. It is now a game, a game between her and these three shadow friends. If she is very still and very quiet maybe, just maybe, they won't find her this time. But her plan does not work. It never does because these three friends have very good noses, maybe even better than her own pink nose. They always smell her in whatever hiding place she is curled up in. The three shadows are very close. Soon these three shadows have twelve feet, and these twelve feet are standing at the edge of her big bush where she is crouched in a tight little ball. She is not afraid, but she still thinks if she is very small and curled up tightly, they won't find her and win the game. Then slowly six big yellow shiny eyes are peering under the bush. These six big shiny yellow eyes are staring right at her beautiful blue eyes, and then they all let out a stifled giggle. And Miss Kitty realizes she has lost once again.

Dolly Doe and her two baby fawns, Lilly and Maggy (short for Magnolia), have found Miss Kitty in her hiding spot—again. They always find Miss Kitty. Of course, it doesn't help that Miss Kitty always hides in the same spot night after night!

Dolly Doe rubs her very wet brown nose against Miss Kitty's wet pink nose. "Hello, Miss Kitty," she says. "Are you doing well this fine warm night?"

"Yes, Dolly, I am very well tonight. In fact, much better tonight than this morning." And Miss Kitty proceeds to tell Dolly Doe all about her morning escapades.

Dolly Doe listens intently while Lilly and Maggy frolic a few feet away on their own. They are happy to be on their own as their mom chats with Miss Kitty. Their mom is a very protective and loving mom. She keeps her two young fawns very close to her at all times, which is very good, but sometimes they do enjoy being away from her watchful eyes, even if only for a few feet. Dolly Doe is a wise doe. She knows what dangers can befall Lilly and Maggy if left unattended too long.

After Dolly Doe hears all about Miss Kitty's early morning misfortunes, she wholeheartedly agrees that Freddy Fox must indeed be taught not to play such mischievous pranks on his friends, not if he wishes to keep those friends. Freddy Fox has pranked all his friends in the woodlands. Maybe it is time for his friends to prank him in return. Dolly Doe gathers Lilly and Maggy close to her side and nods a good night to Miss Kitty.

"We must be on our way and find a midnight snack before the morning sun stops hiding behind the trees," Dolly doe says.

"Good night, Dolly Doe. We will play hide-and-smell another night," says Miss Kitty.

Dolly Doe, with Lilly and Maggy close in step, tiptoes off as one into the woodland shadows as silently as they had appeared. Soon they are covered completely by the shadows until all the shadows look as one.

Miss Kitty continues on her way around her castle. Before long she is back to her great porch and her red cushioned throne. She jumps back up and settles into a tight ball to finish her nightly catnap and then wakes up to another beautiful sunny, warm morning and a fresh bowl of tiny bits of fish, chicken, and beef.

About the Author

MarySue Peters was born and raised in Memphis in 1958. She graduated from Memphis State University (now University of Memphis) in 1980 with an MBA in accounting. After working in the accounting field for ten years, she then started a career with the USPS as a letter carrier. She has one son, who is an RN. Now retired after twenty-eight years of postal service, she and her husband, Claude, currently reside in the small, quiet little country town of Crenshaw, Mississippi. This is her first publication as she embarks on a new adventure of her own.

J

CPSIA information can be obtained
at www.ICGtesting.com
Printed in the USA
JSHW052101030521
14280JS00003B/62

9 781098 061982